DOUBLE TROUBLE

DOUBLE TROUBLE

Adapted by Lexi Ryals

Based on the series created by John D. Beck & Ron Hart

Part One is based on the episode "Sweet 16-A-Rooney," written by Sylvia Green.

Part Two is based on the episode "Dodge-A-Rooney," written by Heather MacGillvray & Linda Mathious.

DISNEP PRESS

Los Angeles • New York

Printed in the United States of America
First Edition, August 2015
1 3 5 7 9 10 8 6 4 2
V475-2873-0-15170

Library of Congress Control Number: 2014952964
ISBN 978-1-4847-1694-6

For more Disney Press fun, visit www.disneybooks.com
Visit DisneyChannel.com

SUSTAINABLE
FORESTRY
INITIATIVE
Certified Chain of Custody
Promoting Sustainable Forestry
www.sfiprogram.org
SFI-01054
The SFI label applies to the text stock

PART
ONE

I had been waiting for that day for, well, forever! Liv Rooney here—actress, singer, star, and twin sister to Maddie Rooney. It was finally time to start planning Maddie's and my sweet sixteen party. To be clear, I'd been planning the party for months already, but it was finally time to put all my plans into action.

So that night after dinner, Maddie and I were ready to go into full party-planning mode.

"One week till our sweet sixteen!" Maddie announced once the table had been cleared.

"After four years of being apart, we are finally together on our birthday! Yay-sies!" I said in a singsong, clapping enthusiastically. I was *so* excited!

"I know." Maddie grinned back at me. "We get to blow out the candles together again."

"Woo-hoo!" Mom hooted. "The three Rooney girls together again and ready to party." Based on the look on Maddie's face, I was pretty sure my mom was doing a dance around the kitchen.

"Liv, don't turn around," Maddie warned, shielding my eyes. "You don't want to see what Mom's doing."

"I don't need to. I can feel the desperation on the back of my neck," I replied.

Mom stopped dancing. "All right, fine. Guess I'll just save my moves for the par-tay."

"Back that party up over here, Kare-bear," Dad hollered.

I needed to move the conversation along pronto, before Mom started dancing again.

"Anyway, so for our party, I have *a few* thoughts," I announced. Then I walked over to the stairs, picked up my stack of "sweet sixteen party" binders, and brought them to the table.

Maddie gave my binders the side eye and raised her hand. "I have *a* thought," she said, pulling a wrinkled orange sticky note from her pocket and smoothing it out on the table.

I wrinkled my nose and opened the top binder. "Okay. So I'm thinking red carpet, designer gowns. We enter Cirque du Soleil–style, spiraling in on silks."

"I'm thinking peanut shells on the floor, steaks the size of our heads. We enter Hungry-Man-style in our casual eating pants," Maddie interrupted, sticking out her stomach and rubbing it like she'd just eaten her weight in steak. She smiled at me as if it was the best idea ever. It wasn't.

"Maddie," I said, trying to be reasonable and pulling on my blond curls, "this is our big one-six. It needs to be epic."

"I know. And I'm thinking epic. There's this new cowboy-jail-themed restaurant—the Hoosegow," Maddie countered, smiling. She tossed her ponytail over her shoulder.

Oh! My! Gosh! She was actually *serious* about this icky cowboy/casual-eating-pants party.

"Wow, we have very different ideas of epic," I said slowly, trying to think of how I could convince her to abandon this gross-tastic idea. I adjusted my black cardigan over my cream lace-peplum top.

"You know what's epic?" Dad asked, slinging one arm around each of us. "Mini-golf birthday parties! They worked for years for you two, ages six to twelve. Done!"

"Dad's right." Mom nodded. "Maddie, you loved it because it was sporty. And there was a castle, so Liv could dress up like a princess. And I loved it because you two were together celebrating your birthday. So, Rooney girls, let's get ready to party!"

"Mom, Mom! Stop," Maddie said desperately.

"Hater," Mom quipped as she turned away.

This was not going *at all* how I had planned. I needed to regain control of this meeting, and fast. After all, you get only one sweet sixteen. It was supposed to be glamorous and fabulous and wondrous—not a mini-golf kiddie party or dinner at a hoosegow, whatever that was.

"As much fun as mini golf was, we're turning sixteen now and we can plan our own party. So, Maddie, let's figure this out. Nothing's been set in stone," I said, laughing nervously.

Just then, Joey pushed his way through the kitchen door, wrapped almost head to toe in bright red silk.

"Liv, I picked up the silks for your epic party entrance," he announced. "Epically bad decision to bring them home on my bike." Then he hopped up the stairs, leaving a long trail of silk behind him.

I gave Maddie my most charming smile, but, clearly, that was *not* going to work, since I could practically see the steam coming out of her ears.

"The silks have already been ordered? You've already planned *our* entire party, haven't you?!" she yelled.

I threw my hands up. "Well, it's not like I can leave it up to you! Casual eating pants?!"

"Spiraling in on silks?!" Maddie countered, making a disgusted face.

"You're being impossible!" I huffed.

"I wish we could just have separate birthdays!" she shouted back.

"Girls!" Mom said firmly, putting herself between us.

"*Uch!*" Maddie snorted and stormed off into the living room.

"*Uch!*" I responded, crossing my arms.

Just then, Joey's bike slammed into the kitchen door, rattling the windows. It must have been tangled in the other end of the silk Joey was wrapped up in. A second later the silk trailing up the stairs went totally taut, and Joey got pulled back down the stairs and collapsed onto the landing.

"Little help?" Joey asked.

Maddie

The next afternoon my mom grabbed Liv and me as soon as we walked into the kitchen after my basketball game—we won, of course, and guess who the MVP was? Yep, it was me. *Bam!* What?!

Anyway, Mom made us cover our eyes, and she brought us into the living room for some surprise. Liv and I still weren't talking, so I wasn't thrilled about any surprise that involved her, but I was trying to be a good sport, since Mom seemed so excited.

She had us stand back-to-back and then launched into a speech: "My twins can't have separate parties on their sweet sixteen. So while you two were at Maddie's basketball game, I came up with something I call a *mom*promise. Take a look."

I opened my eyes to see that Mom had turned our living room into a super-fun-looking rodeo party. There were bales of hay for guests to sit on; the couches and chairs were covered in cowboy-themed fabric; a wagon wheel was propped up by the window; and there was even a cow-print banner over the mantel.

"Dazzleberry!" Liv exclaimed from behind me. Well, that was a relief: she liked it, too.

"Awesome!" I yelled, jumping up and down a little. This party was going to be so fun—and it all felt totally me.

"Hold on," Mom said. "You haven't seen the best part. Turn around."

I turned around, expecting to see more rodeo stuff, but instead I saw what looked like the red carpet to a Hollywood premiere. No wonder Liv had been okay with the decorations: she had been looking at an entirely different setup. Well, it wasn't my first choice, but this way we both got what we wanted.

"Two themes, one party!" Mom announced, sounding delighted with herself.

"It's a red-carpet rodeo!" Dad added. He was standing next to a karaoke machine by the windows and messing with the microphone. "Hey, why isn't this thing working?"

"Maddie, honey, you wanted to go to the Hoosegow, so we're going to have a western barbecue right here in the house," Mom explained. "Joey?"

"Mom, I don't want to say it." Joey pouted. He was dressed as a cowboy—complete with boots, a hat, a leather vest covered in gold-star pins, and chaps.

"Oh, come on, say it!" Mom insisted.

"Yee-haw," he muttered in a monotone voice. I snort-laughed. Joey looked miserable.

"And, Liv, you wanted a Cirque du Soleil red-carpet gala. I give you . . . Parker-razzi!" Mom continued, gesturing to Parker.

"Liv Rooney, Liv Rooney! Who are you wearing?" Parker yelled, snapping pictures of Liv.

Liv immediately started posing for Parker. "Boom, boom, boom—send!" she squealed. Then she turned toward us and smiled. "Mom, this is great. I think we're halfway there—the half that doesn't look like a barn. So I think we should clear out these hay bales and all the barbecue-y stuff, and I just really want to class this place up. I'm thinking we bring in some French contortionists—"

"Why are you tossing out everything I like?" I interrupted. I couldn't believe her! "I thought this was our party."

"Honey, it's time to come clean," Dad hissed to Mom. He was still trying to fix the microphone. "We've kept this secret for way too long."

Mom whispered back, "No, Pete, I'm not telling them"—at the same time Dad finally hit the microphone's ON button—"that they were born on separate days."

My mouth dropped open. I turned to stare at my parents, but I couldn't get words to come out. This made no sense. Twins couldn't be born on different days, right?

Mom laughed nervously and then started singing, *"Camptown ladies sing this song. Doo-dah! Doo-dah!"*

She paused and smiled weakly at us. "This karaoke thing works great. Who's next?"

"What did you just say?!" Liv demanded.

"We have different birthdays?" I asked, stepping forward to stand shoulder to shoulder with Liv. Our fight was suddenly the last thing I cared about.

"Girls, your mother and I have something to tell you," Dad said gently. Then he nudged Mom. "Go ahead, honey."

"Coward," she whispered at him. Then she turned to us and threw up her hands. "Liv, Maddie, the day you were born was truly the greatest day of my life."

"Hey!" Joey exclaimed. "Well, that feels nice."

But Mom just ignored him. "But it actually was the *days* you were born. You see, Liv, you were born on the fifth at eleven fifty-six P.M. But, Maddie, honey, you were born at twelve oh two. On the sixth."

"I was born on the sixth?" I felt like I'd been dipped in icy water. That couldn't be right—it just couldn't. I pointed at the big five on my basketball jersey. "But . . . I mean . . . five's my number because I was born on the fifth. I'm a five."

"Apparently I'm a zero," Joey inserted.

"Wait," Liv interrupted. "Maddie's never celebrated on her actual birthday?" Liv and I exchanged looks. This was so messed up.

"What kind of parents are you?!" Parker yelled, coming to stand next to us. "This is preposterous! I say again, preposterous!"

"Parker, this isn't about you," Dad said sternly.

"It's about all of us," Parker replied, and then turned to us. "If they can do this to her, what does that mean for everybody else? Am I six? Am I eleven? I could be nine."

I shook my head and trudged up to my room. I had a lot to think about.

I was leaning against my bed, trying to process my new identity as a six, when Mom came in and sat down on Liv's bed.

"Hey," Mom said.

"Hey," I answered. I threw my basketball into the air and caught it.

Mom sighed. "Maddie, honey, I'm so sorry. You

know, every year your birthday would roll around and I'd get so excited at the thought of you sitting together, blowing out your birthday candles."

"Then why did you use those trick candles that wouldn't blow out?" I asked, raising one eyebrow.

She thought for a moment and then shrugged. "We wanted the moment to last forever. Plus, a joint birthday party is double the fun." She paused and then threw up her hands. "And it's also half the work. See, I'm trying to be totally honest with you from now on."

I snort-laughed but quickly stopped myself. "Don't be funny. I'm still trying to be mad," I scolded Mom.

"I get that," she said. "Your dad wanted to tell you years ago. But when you were little, you and Liv were inseparable. And as your mother, it just felt wrong to take your special day away."

I raised my eyebrows at her. "Are you seriously trying to take credit for being a good mom right now?"

This time it was Mom who snort-laughed. "Yes, I tried to slip that in. Just tell me what you want to do for your birthday and your father and I will make it happen. Sky's the limit." She paused. "Okay, there's a budget. Again, just being totally honest."

I shook my head. "Thanks, Mom, but honestly, the last thing I want to do right now is celebrate my birthday. I don't think I want to have a party at all this year. I'm sure Liv feels the same way, too."

Mom gave me a hug. "Well, think about it. In the meantime, I made your favorite dinner, chicken potpie." She sighed. "Okay, I didn't make it. It's frozen, out of a box. Woo, the truth really will set you free!"

The next day I called our family, plus Maddie's boyfriend, Diggie, and Maddie's best friends, Stains and Willow, together for a meeting. I clapped my hands as the last of them walked into the living room. "Everyone find a seat. Maddie's off on a run. I bought us some time. She always runs till the end of her playlist, so I added six songs."

"Hey, Joey, I got a spot for you right here," Willow called out from the sofa. She shoved Stains right off the cushion to make room for Joey next to her. Willow has had a hopeless crush on Joey for as long as we've known her. Unfortunately, he does not feel the same way. I wasn't sure who I felt worse for: poor desperate Willow or poor harassed Joey. It was a total crush fail!

"I'm going to say yes because I'm scared to say no," Joey said, cringing as he sat down and Willow scooted as close to him as she could get, pinning him against the arm of the couch. "Ow."

"Okay! You are all here because you are Maddie's best friends and family," I explained. "I want you to help me throw a surprise party for her. You have to keep it a secret." I turned to Mom and Dad and gave them a look—their lie still wasn't excused as far as I was concerned. "I know that won't be a problem for you two."

"Mom said Maddie doesn't even want a party this year," Joey protested. "Also, I cannot feel my ribs."

"I can," Willow said dreamily.

"Maddie says she doesn't want a party, but I know my sister better. This birthday bombshell has knocked her for a loop, and we're going to fix it," I pressed on.

"That's very sweet," Mom said.

"We'll do anything to help," Dad added.

Parker laughed. "Of course you will. You're totally on the hook for this."

"Well, I'm in," Diggie piped up. "I want to make Maddie's sweet sixteen as amazing as it can be."

"Careful," Dad said, giving Diggie his sternest look.

"Right," Diggie said with a cringe. "Sorry." Poor Diggie was so intimidated by our dad. It was kinda adorable how much he wanted Dad to like him for Maddie's sake. Maddie was lucky to have such a good boyfriend.

"Maddie's never had her birthday on her actual day, so I want to give her a party she'll never forget," I said. Now that everyone was on board, it was time to outline the rest of my plan.

"You rock, Liv. I have eight sisters and all I got for my last birthday was a comb. It's a nice one, though," Stains said, pulling a comb out and running it through her hair. "Unbreakable. See?" She bent the comb, and it immediately snapped in half. She moaned, "Aw, man."

I shook my head. Keeping this group on track was like herding cats. "Willow, Diggie, Stains? You're going to take Maddie to the Hoosegow on Saturday while the rest of us get the house ready for the party. Do not bring her home until midnight. That's when her actual birthday begins."

"Midnight? Isn't that awfully late for a party?" Mom protested.

"You mean like sixteen years late, Mom?" I replied pointedly.

She cringed. "Midnight party? Fun!"

We stayed until we'd worked out all the details. Joey's job was to goad Maddie into throwing herself a party at the Hoosegow. Maddie's friends and Diggie all had to pretend they had plans Sunday so that Maddie would be forced to do her party on Saturday night. They aren't great actors, so this was the riskiest part of the plan, but I knew they would try their best. The rest of us would set up for the big surprise! I'd been excited about *my* sweet sixteen, but I was even more excited to give Maddie the most surprise-tastic party ever!

The next day I hid around the corner from our lockers and watched as the first part of my plan started. Right on schedule, a contortionist delivered Maddie's and Joey's invitations to my fake Cirque du Soleil gala.

See, it was crucial that Maddie think I was throwing a party for myself so she'd get mad enough to blow off my party and stay away, giving us time to set up for her surprise party. And it was working like a charm. I watched as she stormed down the hall to her friends and invited them all to the Hoosegow.

Snap! The jaws of my trap-tastic plan had closed! Maddie hated me. Hello, best sister everrrr!

Maddie

I still wasn't feeling much like celebrating on Monday when we headed back to school. Even an extra-long jog on Sunday hadn't cheered me up—and I still couldn't figure out how all those super-long reggae songs had ended up on my workout playlist.

My first stop at school was my locker. I was on a mission to update all the fives in my life to sixes, using electrical tape.

"Hey, Maddie. What are you doing?" Joey asked, leaning up against the locker next to mine. He was the only one of my siblings who really seemed to notice

I'd been in a funk since Mom and Dad had told us the truth about my birthday.

"I'm changing all my lucky fives into sixes," I said, opening my locker door to show him the ridiculous number of fives decorating the inside. "Turns out in the first fifteen years of my life, I stuck fives everywhere. Every. Where."

Joey nodded sagely. "Identity crisis. I can relate. I remember that painful transition from Joseph to Joe to Joey, with a brief stint as Baby J, and then ultimately back to Joey."

I laughed. "Wasn't there a J-Dawg in there somewhere?"

"Don't bring that up," Joey said, bristling.

Just then, we were interrupted by the strangest thing I'd ever seen in the halls of Ridgewood High School—a contortionist wearing a multicolored spandex bodysuit, walking along on his hands. His legs were wrapped over his shoulders so he dragged his butt along the floor. Several thick cream envelopes stuck out from between his toes.

"Maddie and Joey Rooney?" the contortionist asked.

I took a step back—I didn't mean to, but he startled me. "Character from my nightmares?" I responded.

"Delivery," he said cheerfully. "Left foot, between the third and fourth toes."

I reached out and took two invitations from between his toes. Then he turned and butt-walked away. I shuddered and handed one to Joey. We both opened the envelopes and pulled out invitations. Joey read, "'You are cordially invited to the Cirque du Soleil red-carpet gala celebrating the sweet sixteen of Liv Rooney.'"

"Liv's throwing a party for herself?!" I yelled. I could *not* believe Liv. I wanted to scream or stomp or crush something, I was so angry. We were supposed to be twins, best friends. If Liv was really my best friend, she would understand how upset I was and skip a party this year, but instead she was selfishly using the fact that I didn't want to celebrate as an excuse to make everything all about her, as usual. I had had just about enough of the famous Liv Rooney.

"Wow," Joey said, raising his eyebrows. "Liv took

this birthday scandal a lot better than you did. Like a lot better. A. Lot."

"I can't believe she just dumped me to do her own thing," I said, fuming.

"Yeah. Does that make you mad?" Joey asked. "I think I'd be mad. I'd be, like, really mad."

I had an idea. "You know what, if Liv's throwing a party for herself, then I'm throwing a party for myself. I'm going to the Hoosegow," I announced. I took off down the hall to Diggie's locker. He was talking to Willow and Stains—perfect.

"Hey, guys, do you want to go out for my birthday? Hoosegow on Sunday, what do you say?" I asked.

"Can't," Willow answered. "We have plans on Sunday." Stains and Diggie nodded.

"What plans?" I asked.

My friends exchanged nervous looks. What was going on?

"I've got a . . ." Willow hesitated, looking around. "Drum circle."

"Washing my ferret," Stains added. I narrowed my eyes. Why did it seem like they were up to something?

"Book club," Diggie replied.

I scoffed. "You're in a book club?"

"Sure," Diggie said with a nod. "Every month we pick a book, then we watch the movie and we talk about it." Okay, that made a lot more sense than my homework-boycotting boyfriend's voluntarily reading. He *did* like movies. I needed to relax. Liv's backstabbing was making me paranoid, but my friends would never do something like that to me.

"We're available Saturday," Stains suggested.

"Saturday?" I asked. "Aren't you guys going to Liv's party?"

Stains shook her head. "Not invited. I guess we didn't make the cut. Liv's loss. We're the cool kids."

Oh, Liv made me so mad. "She's throwing a party for herself and didn't even invite my friends?" I growled. "You know what? I am free on Saturday. We're going to the Hoosegow!"

Finally, Saturday rolled around. I'd spent all week going on and on about details for *my* sweet sixteen, and Maddie was barely talking to me—although she did wish me happy birthday through gritted teeth. Everything was going according to plan! She headed out to the Hoosegow around seven, and the party setup went into high gear.

I'd settled on the perfect theme for Maddie's party—a grown-up mini-golf extravaganza. We were making a nine-hole course in the backyard, with a moat, a windmill, a Hoosegow hole (the things I do for my sister!), and a basketball hole. Plus the party would have Maddie's favorite snacks, a cake, and, of course, all Maddie's friends. The whole thing was Maddie-tastic, if I do say so myself.

Mom was making the cake. I was on decorations—I make a pop-tastic balloon arrangement—and Joey and Dad were setting up the mini-golf course in the backyard. Parker . . . well, who knew what Parker was doing?

A little before ten o'clock I called Diggie to check in.

"This is Jailhouse One, over," he answered. I could hear country music and people chanting, "Stains! Stains!" in the background. I didn't even want to know what that was about.

"Diggie! How's it going?" I asked nervously.

"Great. We're just about to order dessert. She doesn't suspect a thing," he replied.

"Dessert?" I wailed. "You can't be on dessert already. It's barely ten o'clock. You need to keep her out of the house until midnight!" That needed to be the longest dessert in the history of desserts.

"I'll do what I can," he said sheepishly. "But I didn't expect the service to be so fantastic at a restaurant like this."

"I'm trying to do something nice for my sister! Do not make me regret trusting you!" I warned him. Then I hung up the phone. "The fate of my plan rests on someone named Diggie," I muttered to myself.

This was a disaster. I needed to check on the party prep—pronto. If they were going to show up early—which would totally ruin the whole midnight-party-on-Maddie's-*actual*-birthday thing—at least we could be ready for them!

I walked into the kitchen to find Mom frosting the cake and Parker frowning at it.

"A one-layer cake, really?" Parker asked. "You think that's going to make up for sixteen years of fibs and fraud?"

"I was going to put little purple frosting flowers on the corners," Mom said, gesturing to a bag of purple icing.

"Oh, well, that'll impress . . . no one," Parker snapped.

Mom sighed. I could tell she was still feeling really guilty. "I guess I could do a few more layers."

"Yeah, maybe one for every year that you lied,"

Parker said, making a mean face before walking out to the backyard.

"It'll look great, Mom," I said encouragingly, and then hurried after Parker.

"Wow, this mini-golf course actually looks pretty good," Parker said excitedly. And it really did. "I'm glad someone's paying attention to what Liv's trying to pull off here. Let's see that windmill spin."

"Oh, it doesn't actually spin," Dad said.

"It's decorative," Joey added. "Like the treadmill in Mom and Dad's bedroom."

"You've got to be kidding me," Parker exclaimed, throwing up his hands. "A crummy cake and a nonspinny windmill? Liv is trying to re-create the magical mini-golf parties of Maddie's youth. If we're going to do this, we're going to do this right."

"He does have a point," I said, nodding. Then I nudged him. "Even if he isn't being very nice about it."

"I guess we could take apart one of my remote-control cars and use the motor to make it spin," Joey said critically, studying the windmill.

"Yeah, we could do that. We could also play duck,

duck, goose," Parker said sarcastically. "Am I the only one who cares?"

"How 'bout we take apart the riding mower and use the motor from that bad boy?" Dad suggested. I clapped. That would be perfect!

"Now we're talking. Birthday magic, monkeys! Let's go, let's go," Parker said, then nodded and headed back into the house.

"Where are you going?" Dad asked.

"It's already two hours past my bedtime. If I don't take a nap before the party, I'm going to be a real cranky-pants," Parker replied.

Maddie

The Hoosegow was everything I had hoped it would be—brick walls with wood beams, WANTED posters featuring cattle rustlers and stagecoach robbers, peanut shells on the floor, and even a jail cell in the back with a salad bar inside. All the waiters were dressed up like cowboys, and they served all the food in mason jars and rustic baskets.

The food was delicious and they let you eat as much as you wanted. We were all stuffing our faces when Willow came back from her second trip to the salad bar, escorted by our waiter, Tim, who was dressed as the sheriff.

"There you go, little lady," Sheriff Tim said. "You're welcome to as many return visits to the salad bar as you want at the Hoosegow, but only under the watchful eye of the law."

Willow laughed and sat down. She whispered across the table to me, "Watchful eye? Hardly. I filled my whole purse with baby corn."

"Don't mess with Sheriff Tim, Willow," I warned her. "He's packing ketchup *and* mustard. Hey, Sheriff Tim, ketchup me," I said, pointing to my fries.

Sheriff Tim pulled a ketchup bottle out of his belt holster, spun it around, and shot a perfect stream of ketchup onto my plate.

"Whatever's happening at Liv's stupid red-carpet party couldn't be nearly as cool as this. I'd rather be at a place where you can throw your peanut shells on the floor," I told my friends, throwing a handful of shells over my shoulder.

"And rib bones," Stains agreed. She pointed next to her chair, and I must have made a disgusted face, because she winced and asked, "Am I not supposed to do that?"

"Always a lady, Stains," I said, shaking my head. "Always a lady."

Diggie pointed across the restaurant. "Ooh, guys. They're going to arrest someone again."

One of the waiters rang a bell, and a whole posse of waiters led by Sheriff Tim descended on another customer.

"You are under arrest for cattle rustling, stagecoach robbery, and spitting in the presence of a lady," Sheriff Tim announced. The customer held up his hands and let himself be led over to the holding cell with the salad bar inside. Sheriff Tim locked the customer in as everyone cheered.

Just then, Diggie's phone rang. "I gotta take this," he said after looking at the number on the screen. "Book club stuff." He jumped up and hurried away while we watched the jailed customer escape back to his table. This place was the best! It was almost enough to take my mind off the fact that my sister was celebrating her birthday without me.

"Okay, guys," Stains announced, "I'm gonna try the chicken stockade challenge. If anyone can eat an entire chicken in under an hour, it's me. And I really want that cool T-shirt you win if you do it."

"That is awesome!" I encouraged her. "Come on, I'll go with you."

Stains and I headed over to the stockade, and they locked her in and set a huge rotisserie chicken in front of her face. Sheriff Tim started the clock, and Stains tore into that chicken like a wild animal. She couldn't use her hands, since they were trapped in the stockade. It got messy fast.

I saw Diggie return to the table, and Willow pointed at us.

"Wipe!" Stains ordered. I pulled my attention back to her and got a wet wipe ready.

I started to reach toward her face with the wipe and then stopped. I didn't want to put my hands in her chomp zone. "You know what? Let's just hose you off when this is over."

One hour later, Stains was wearing a brand-new Hoosegow T-shirt. Unsurprisingly, it was already stained.

"Good job, Stains. I've never been more impressed or disgusted," I said as we sat back down at our table.

"You know, you didn't have to eat the bones to win the shirt," Diggie told her.

"When I commit, I commit, man," Stains replied.

Sheriff Tim walked over carrying a cupcake with a candle in it. "We hear it's your birthday, little lady." He set the cupcake in front of me.

"Uh, it's not actually my birthday until midnight," I told him.

"Well, blow out the candle," he replied. "It's somebody's birthday."

I stared down at the candle for a minute, but I just couldn't bring myself to blow it out.

"Go ahead. Make a wish, Maddie," Diggie encouraged me.

"I can't. Sheriff Tim's right. It is somebody's birthday—Liv's," I told my friends, shaking my head. "And the only wish that's popping into my head is that I wish we were blowing out our candles together."

"That's so sweet!" Willow cooed. "Let's get you home right now!"

Stains reached over and smacked the back of Willow's head.

"Yeah, let's go," I announced. I checked the time. It was already eleven o'clock. If we hurried, we might still make the end of Liv's party. I just hoped she'd forgive me for missing most of it. "Come on, guys, get up."

"You sure?" Diggie asked. "We've barely been here four hours."

I stood up to go. Just then, a waiter rang the bell for another arrest. The posse approached the girl sitting at the table next to ours.

Sheriff Tim announced, "You are under arrest for cattle rustling—"

But Diggie jumped up before he could finish his speech and yelled, "You're arresting the wrong bandit!" Then he pointed at me. "This girl right here, she's the cattle rustler."

"Yeah, man, lock her up!" Stains yelled.

"What are you guys doing?" I hissed at them.

"Lock her up! Lock her up!" Willow chanted. Soon everyone in the Hoosegow had joined her.

Sheriff Tim shrugged, grabbed me, and led me over to the holding cell. Then he locked me inside with the salad.

"Hey! Let me out of here! I've got to get to Liv's party before it's over!" I yelled at my friends. What was with them?

"Good move, Diggie," Stains said, and high-fived him.

Luckily, it wasn't a real jail cell. I reached through the bars, snagged the keys from a hook on the wall, unlocked the door, and walked out.

"Yeah, I'm pretty smooth under pressure. There's a new sheriff in town, and his name is Diggie, and he's the meanest sheriff on Earth," Diggie bragged to Stains and Willow, not knowing I had escaped.

I reached out and tapped him on the shoulder. He jumped about a foot in the air and turned around sheepishly. "We're outta here," I announced, and then I turned and stomped out to the car. I didn't know what was up with my friends, but they were not keeping me away from Liv.

Maddie

At 11:55, I heard Diggie's car pull into the driveway. Thank goodness he'd managed to stall for more time. Everything was ready—I couldn't wait to see Maddie's face when we yelled "Surprise!"

"It's midnight," I heard Maddie saying from our porch. "Seriously, Diggie? Sixteen wrong turns? And I've never heard of a law that says you have to go five miles an hour past a graveyard."

"That's just showing respect, man," Stains said, defending him.

"I don't hear any music, and the red carpet's rolled up. I totally missed Liv's party," Maddie said. She sounded bummed.

"Okay, places, everyone," I called softly. I waited until everyone had hidden, and then I switched off the backyard lights and crouched down under the light switch. I could hear Maddie and her friends talking as they walked through the house.

"Su—" Stains, Willow, and Diggie all started.

Oops! I guess I forgot to tell them we'd be hiding in the back.

"—upper was really nice at the Hoosegow," Diggie finished.

"Where is everybody?" Maddie asked. I could hear her walking into the kitchen.

"Su—" Stains, Willow, and Diggie all started again as they followed her.

"—omebody give me a 'what-what?'" Willow said in a weird high-pitched voice.

"I don't think anyone's home. Are the cars here?" Maddie asked, sounding panicked.

Finally, Maddie burst through the back door. I flipped the switch, lighting up the backyard, and we all jumped out.

"Surprise!" everyone yelled. I sang it, of course, but

Joey
7d ago

Our parents tried to distract us with a weird song. #nicetry

Liv
6d ago

I came up with the perfect plan to surprise Maddie. #imagenius

Parker
6d ago

These family meetings are always so awkward.
#willowandjoey #livhasideas #drama

Maddie
5d ago

I just got invited to my twin sister's birthday party—that she's having without me.
#sorude

Maddie
3d ago

My idea of a party: good friends, huge steaks, and my eating pants. You gotta love it.

Maddie
3d ago

ROTISSERIE CHICKEN STOCKADE CHALLENGE
THE HOOSEGOW

If anyone can eat a whole chicken with no hands, it's Stains. #eventhebones

Parker & Joey
3d ago

We had to get this windmill to spin, so obviously a lawn-mower motor was the solution.

Maddie
3d ago

Even though she sometimes makes me really mad, I just couldn't blow out my birthday candle without Liv.

Maddie
4h ago

Liv and I are both here. Um, what?!
#fakehappy

Maddie
3h ago

Why do I hear a conga line? That's never a good thing.

Look, everyone, it's the Golden Chords, my all-oldie performance troupe. #Jazzleberry!

Word to your mothers, y'all.

Maddie
3h ago

This crowded room is tighter than Budge's workout pants. #burn

Liv
2h ago

Shoulda stuck with shuffleboard, granny, 'cause this game's gonna hurt.

Maddie
2h ago

We decided to make it a real competition.
#throwdown #sorryLiv

Maddie
1h ago

I was ready for a dodgeball riot. #ohsnap

I don't even think she could hear my perfect pitch over her friends' yelling.

Maddie's mouth dropped open and she looked beyond shocked—it was perfect!

Stains, Diggie, and Willow hurried through the door. Stains sighed. "We missed saying 'surprise'?! You gotta be kidding me!"

"Happy sweet sixteen, Maddie!" I said, stepping forward to wrap my sister in a hug. She looked so cute in her dark jeans and ombré blouse. She even had her hair down for once.

"Wait, this is for me? Where's your red-carpet party?" Maddie asked.

I laughed. "There was no party. I totally played you, but don't feel bad. I *am* a day older."

Maddie laughed, too. She turned to Diggie, Stains, and Willow and shook her head at them.

"Hi, remember us? The ones you were screaming at the whole way past the graveyard?" Diggie asked her, smiling. I wasn't sure what they'd been doing at a graveyard; later I was going to need to get the whole story on how they managed to kill so much time.

"You guys were all in on it?" Maddie asked. "Everything you did tonight was just to keep me from getting home?"

They nodded. "Well, not everything," Stains admitted. "I really wanted this T-shirt."

Maddie turned back to me and gave me another hug. "Aw, mini golf. Just like the old days. That's so sweet."

"We got so wrapped up in what kind of party we each wanted that we forgot the best part is getting to do it together," I explained. "There was no way I was going to let you skip out on celebrating your birthday this year, so I made the perfect party for you!"

Mom gestured to the cake. "Someone made you a cake," she announced.

"A basketball cake? This is amazing," Maddie said, walking over and studying the layers of icing and the perfect basketball on the top.

"Sixteen layers of buttercream and guilt," Mom explained. "Mama's done her time. We're moving on. The Rooney girls are ready to get their party on!" She smiled and then busted into her dance moves.

"Mom, we've forgiven you. Stop punishing us," Maddie said, shaking her head at Mom's moves.

"Maddie, we even got you a number six jersey because we figured you'd want to change your number," Dad said. He held up a brand-new Ridgewood High jersey with a perfect number six on it.

"Actually," Maddie said. "I've decided to stick with number five. That's the day my best friend was born."

We smiled at each other while Mom lit the candles on Maddie's cake.

"Liv, get over here and help me blow out all these candles," Maddie said.

"Hang on, I want to get a video. I left my phone in the garage when I was grabbing decorations," I called back as I hurried into the garage to find my phone.

Maddie

Liv left to get her phone, and Parker perked up. "Video?" he asked. "Then we've gotta have the windmill going! Dad, turn it on."

Dad held up a remote and pushed a button. The windmill blades began to spin slowly.

"Oh, I love it!" I cried. It was just like the mini-golf course we went to when we were little. My family had really outdone themselves.

"We did a good thing today, boys," Dad said, putting one arm around Parker and the other around Joey.

"See what happens when you listen to Parker?" Parker said with a smirk.

Just then, the blades on the windmill started spinning faster and faster.

"That thing kicks up quite a breeze," Joey mused.

Napkins, cups, and plates blew off the snack table. The lawn furniture edged slowly toward the garage. Everyone's hair whipped around. Even the cake was shaking on its stand. This wasn't a breeze—it was turning into a full-force wind tunnel.

"We gotta turn it off!" I cried.

"Don't worry, birthday girl. Your hero's here!" Diggie called, and ran toward the windmill as fast as he could—which wasn't that fast, considering he was being blown backward. As he tried to get closer, the cake lost its battle with the wind. It went flying, covering everyone in frosting.

"Hey, superhero," I called as Diggie reached the windmill. "The plug's right here." I unplugged the cord, and the wind stopped suddenly. Diggie ran into the windmill and fell backward, and the rest of the guests started trying to straighten their disheveled hair and clothes.

"Whoa . . ." Willow said, looking around at the chaos.

"Nice work on the cake, Mom," Parker said, licking some frosting off his arm.

Liv opened the garage door and stepped out into the mess. She looked around and sighed. "Oh, dear. Well, sweet seventeen has a nice ring to it, too."

I just laughed. I didn't care one bit that the food and cake were ruined. This was hands down the best birthday I'd ever had—all thanks to my twin sis.

PART

TWO ♥

Maddie

After a totally awesome afternoon, I sailed into the kitchen, where Mom was making dinner. "I had the best day doing community service at the senior center!" I announced, leaning against the kitchen counter. "Helping people feels great."

I knew Mom would be excited for me; after all, she's the chair of the Ridgewood High Community Service campaign. It was all thanks to her that I'd started volunteering to teach the Silver Steppers workout program at the senior center.

"I'm so glad, Maddie," she replied, stirring a pot on the stove. "Would you help me set the table?"

I shook my head and sighed loudly. "Ugh, I'm *so* tired."

Mom shook her head but let me rest. "I'm really proud of you and your sister. But I'm surprised you two didn't pick the same project."

"Liv knows the senior center is my turf. I've been there for two years. Plus, it's all fluorescent lighting. She says it makes her look like she has the flu," I responded with a shrug.

Mom smiled. "Well, she was unbelievably excited about volunteering for Beautify Wisconsin."

"Yeah, wait till she finds out what 'Beautify Wisconsin' actually means," I said, trying not to laugh. I flipped my ponytail over my shoulder and adjusted my charm bracelet.

Just then, the back door banged open and Liv clomped in. She was wearing a neon-orange reflective vest over one of her adorable outfits, and she was absolutely covered in dirt and grime. Her usually perfect bouncy hair was flattened and limp, and there was an old straw sticking out of it. She was still holding her litter stick, with a crumpled cup stuck on the end of it.

"Whoa. Did you . . . change your hair?" Mom asked, trying not to laugh.

"Turns out Beautify Wisconsin is *not* going door-to-door, giving makeovers. I spent two hours in a ditch picking up anything people threw out of their cars: cigarette butts, potato chip bags, and, most humiliating of all," Liv replied with a sniff, "a season-one DVD of *Sing It Loud!*" Liv sobbed quietly, holding up a dirty and dented DVD case.

I was shocked. Liv didn't even sing the show's title, which could only mean one thing: Liv was feeling *seriously* low. This did not bode well for her volunteering days. Too bad she hadn't lucked out like me and gotten the perfect assignment! *Bam!* What?!

Joey

It felt like an important day, because it was: the day Joey Rooney made a name for himself, one that wasn't "Liv and Maddie's little brother." I was finally going to grab some glory for myself. I hurried over to the huge bronze statue of Paulie the Porcupine, our school's mascot, which sits in the school foyer. The varsity boys' basketball team and the entire pep club were waiting there.

"All right, Fighting Porcupines, listen up!" Diggie, Maddie's boyfriend and captain of the boys' basketball team, announced as I arrived and stood next to my friend Skippy. "Friday night we play our biggest rivals, the Fairview Tiger Sharks. And those dirty Tiger

Sharks are going to try to steal our beloved mascot, Paulie the Porcupine. Every year, two freshmen are chosen to watch over Paulie the night before the big game. As basketball team captain, I have selected Joey Rooney and Skippy Ramirez to keep Paulie safe from the Tiger Sharks!"

The crowd booed. I exchanged nervous looks with Skippy. "Just to be clear, are you booing us or the Tiger Sharks?" I asked.

The crowd booed again.

"Stop saying 'Tiger Sharks,'" Skippy hissed nervously.

The crowd booed as soon as they heard the word *tiger*. So I decided to try again. "We're your Paulie protectors!" I announced.

The crowd cheered, and I breathed a sigh of relief. At least they weren't against Skippy and me from the start. See, the Fairview Tiger Sharks have an actual shark tank. On game day, they throw in chum to whip the fans into a frenzy. At our school we hang meat around a porcupine's neck for luck. Yeah, we pretty much have the worst mascot ever. But I had begged

Diggie for the job. If Skippy and I could keep Paulie safe all night, we'd get the honor of hanging the first bratwurst link around Paulie's neck. It's like winning an Olympic medal, but with meat. And then no one would ever forget the name Joey Rooney!

Liv

I may have hated my community service project, but Maddie definitely didn't hate hers. She hadn't stopped talking about how much fun she had teaching a group of little old ladies how to exercise at the senior center. She called them the Silver Steppers—totally adorbs, right? So, since the lady from Beautify Wisconsin had totally yelled at me when I called and suggested we start a makeover division for people instead of parks and roadsides, I figured I'd tag along with Maddie and see if I could volunteer at the senior center. Old people love me, and I was highly unlikely to end up covered in roadside filth that way.

So the next afternoon I put on my most capable-looking volunteer outfit and headed over to the senior center. I found Maddie teaching her exercise class in a big room. It was so cute! She had the Silver Steppers sitting in rolling chairs and working with weights. Every minute or so, Maddie would blow her whistle and they would roll to the next station. I waited until they had just swapped stations and walked on over.

"Maddie!" I yelled, waving. This was going to be *so* much fun.

"Who's Maddie?" an old lady in a leotard and pleated skirt asked.

Maddie looked so surprised to see me. Yay-sies! I love surprising Maddie. "Liv? What are you doing here?!" she asked.

"I've decided to ditch the ditch," I announced. Then I realized what I'd just said. I giggled and twirled a strand of hair around my finger. "I didn't even know I was going to say that until it came out. I'm adorable. *Anyway*, I'm shopping for a new community service idea and—"

"You can't volunteer here," Maddie interrupted. Wait a second, did she not want me there? But before I could ask, she hurried to say, "I already asked.

There's a waiting list. Talk to Mom. She'll reassign you. Really would love it if we could do this together, but we can't. Bummer. So sad."

My sister was the best. She knew how much I hated the ditch, so she had already tried to get us together! Awww! The thing is, Maddie isn't always the most persuasive. I bet they would find me an opening if I talked to them. I just needed to turn on the Liv Rooney charm!

Parker

My dad spent all afternoon putting together his new grill. I waited until he was done to go anywhere near the backyard so that he didn't draft me into helping him. I had no desire to be his tool monkey for hours. Luckily, I arrived home just as he tightened his last bolt and was showing it off to Mom.

"Check it out. The Fire Magic Smokehouse Deluxe is ready for action, complete with thumbprint ignition pad. I'm the only one who can use it," Dad announced.

Mom laughed. "Oh, I must have one of those on the stove, the dishwasher, the dryer, the iron, the vacuum, and the toilet handle after Parker uses it," she joked. But when Dad didn't laugh, she hurried on. "Sorry. That's some grill! Please tell me more."

"This baby's been banned in the States. They say the hydrogen fuel cell is too 'experimental.' I had to ship it piece by piece from Laos," Dad explained proudly.

I decided to interrupt before I had to hear any more. "My scooter broke," I announced, holding up the two pieces for them to see. "It was the weirdest thing. Me and Cooper and Isaac and Kalden and Jack and Richie and Stevie and Evan were riding on it and it just snapped. Piece of junk."

Mom raised an eyebrow. "Eight people on a scooter? What were you thinking?!"

"We were going for the world record," I explained. "Didn't think it would snap till we added Big Wayne. So, can you glue it back together?"

Dad shook his head. "Sorry, buddy, they haven't invented a glue strong enough to fix that," he said.

That sounded like a challenge to me. "Correction. They haven't invented it *yet*. To my laboratory!" I exclaimed, and headed toward the kitchen.

"Was it a mistake putting him in advanced science classes?" I heard Dad ask Mom.

"When you find your kid trying to build himself a robotic third arm, you do what you can to keep his mind focused on good and not evil," Mom said, shaking her head as I walked through the door.

I knew just what to try first. This was going to be fun!

Joey

I could not wait to start our Paulie watch. Skippy and I had packed everything we might need to defend Paulie and were ready for our twenty-four-hour vigil. The boys' basketball team was waiting for us when we got there.

Diggie kept it short and sweet. He said, "Look, dude. Just make sure nothing happens to Paulie. He's our good luck charm."

"I'll crush anyone who comes near him," Skippy said eagerly. I know this is hard to believe, but Skippy is actually scrawnier than me.

Diggie raised an eyebrow and turned to me. "Okay, Joey, I can't believe I'm saying this, but I think you're the muscle."

I couldn't believe it—*I was the muscle!* Which came with great responsibility. At least, I thought it did. I didn't know; I'd never been the muscle before!

"Joey, thanks for hooking me up with this job. This is going to be so much fun," Skippy announced happily.

"Fun? This is serious work. Have you looked around? We can't secure this porcupine. I did a quick three-sixty and saw forty-seven possible points of entry," I told him a little frantically. "Forty-eight if those Tiger Sharks can tunnel up through the floors."

Skippy looked terrified. "This is bad. We'll be the freshmen that let Paulie fall into enemy hands. What are we going to do? We need a new plan!" he wailed.

I nodded. "Give me a second, I'm thinking," I told him.

Skippy stepped forward and stared at me, waiting for instructions.

I pushed him back. "Don't look me in the eye when I'm thinking. It makes me uncomfortable." After a few moments, I had an idea. "Okay, Skippy, this is what we're going to do. . . ."

Maddie

The next afternoon I was leading my Silver Steppers in a round of jumping jacks before strength training. "Four more. Three, two, one, and take a break."

Everyone stopped except Budge, who just kept jumping.

"Don't need a break. Thanks to you and my titanium hips, I'm practically bionic," Budge announced. I loved seeing my seniors as excited about exercise as I was.

I laughed. "Let's not exaggerate things, Budge. You did need me to unscrew your water bottle."

She winked at me. "I can do that myself. But you

could use the exercise. I'm looking out for you, hon. You're the best thing to hit the wrinkle ranch since Ralphie showed up in short shorts."

Just then, a commotion at the door caught my attention. A whole line of seniors was dancing into the room in a conga line.

"*Cha-cha-cha-cha! Hey! Cha-cha-cha-cha!*" they sang as they snaked through the room. Finally, I saw Liv at the end of the line. I groaned.

"And big finish," Liv called. "Jazz hands!" The line broke apart, and all the dancers posed with jazz hands. "Surprise-ies!" Liv said in a singsong as she bounced over to me.

"Liv. What are you doing here?" I asked through gritted teeth.

"I'm teaching show choir. I stopped at the office and it turns out they do have room for volunteers," she explained. Then she gestured to her seniors. "Say hello to the Golden Chords." Of course she sang "the Golden Chords."

"*Hello,*" the group sang. Liv joined in and carried her "hello" out with a diva-esque flourish.

The gentleman who had been leading the conga

line stepped forward and looked me over. "Hello," he said suavely. "Am I seeing double, or did I lose a contact? Baxter Fontanel. Charmed." I couldn't help laughing. Wearing pressed trousers and a jaunty cap and holding his smart cane, he was clearly a charmer.

"Baxter, put the piano in the corner," Liv said sweetly.

"Sure, send the seventy-year-old man with the cane to move the piano," he grumbled, but hurried off to do what Liv had asked anyway.

"Wait. You're going to practice here?" I asked, confused. "But this is my room."

Liv nodded. "The other rooms are booked. I thought it would be fun to share. Just another twinsie thing we can do together. So exciting, right?" Liv continued, oblivious to the panic on my face.

How do you tell your best friend to go back to the ditch she came from? You tell her the cold, hard truth. Or . . . you totally chicken out.

"I am so glad you're here. Jazz hands," I said weakly, making the least enthusiastic jazz hands ever. Liv jumped up and down, delighted.

"Jazz hands!" she exclaimed.

Joey

I finished tying a knot in the rope around the tree in our backyard and looked up with a huge smile on my face.

"Bro, getting Paulie out of that hot zone was a stroke of pure genius," Skippy congratulated me. "But are you sure this is the best hiding spot?"

I was pretty proud of myself, to be honest. "Absolutely." I pointed up to where Paulie was hanging from a rope looped around a high branch of a large tree. He dangled about eight feet above our back patio. "He'll be safe until tomorrow." There was no way those Tiger Sharks were going to find Paulie now.

"Are you sure your parents aren't going to notice a

giant porcupine swinging from their oak tree?" Skippy asked.

"No way. Everybody's got their nose in their phones nowadays. Nobody looks up," I assured him, pushing my glasses up on my nose.

Just then, my mom and dad walked out from the garage. They were both so busy looking at their phones that Mom bumped right into me.

"Oops. Didn't see you there. I'm watching a kitten video!" Mom exclaimed. Then she said in a baby voice to her phone, "You should've known you weren't big enough to jump over that baby gate."

"Joey," Dad said seriously. "I need some answers from you and I need them now."

Skippy and I both cringed. He must have seen Paulie.

"Bratwurst or pork burgers for the barbecue this weekend?" Dad asked, gesturing to his brand-new, super-expensive grill. "I know I'm asking early, but I hate having things hanging over my head."

I gave a sigh of relief. "Well, Dad. Just pick a dead animal and I'll eat it."

"My man." Dad smiled and gave me a high five. Then he looked over at Mom. "Does it look like rain?"

Please don't look up! I thought frantically.

"Good question. Let me check my phone," Mom replied, and immediately started typing furiously as they walked into the house.

I let out a breath I hadn't realized I was holding. We'd made it through one encounter with no one noticing Paulie. "Huh? What's that? Who's a Paulie protector? This guy," I chanted. "It's gonna be awesome when we hang that first bratwurst on Paulie. Everyone will be clapping, and just when they think we can't get any cooler . . ."

Skippy and I both unzipped our hoodies to reveal the awesome T-shirts we'd made. My teal shirt said BOO on the front, and Skippy's orange shirt said YAH. "Boo-yah!" we exclaimed together.

I smiled. "Perfect. Remember to stay on my left. We want to be 'boo-yah.' 'Yah-boo' is just stupid."

Parker

My parents have no faith in my abilities, I swear. They were constantly checking up on me and asking if I was making progress—no faith, no faith at all. Of course, Mom may have just wanted her kitchen back. I'd kind of taken it over, but it was all going to be worth it, since I was pretty sure this batch of glue was *the one*. I had my lab goggles on and was mixing chemicals in several different beakers. The yellow frothy one was coming along nicely. I was about to test it when Mom and Dad walked in.

"How's it going with the glue, Professor?" Dad asked.

I sighed. "Did people ask Einstein 'how's it going' while he was splitting atoms?"

Dad raised an eyebrow. "Um, Einstein never split an atom."

"Maybe that's because people kept interrupting him!" I exclaimed. I inspected my neon-yellow foam—it looked perfect. I took a tiny dab and stuck it to the bottom of a pan drying in the dish rack. Then I walked over to the refrigerator door and pressed the bottom of the pan against it. "Now the moment of truth." I let go cautiously, and it stuck! "Yes! It worked."

Dad walked over and pulled on the pan. The refrigerator door came open but the pan didn't move. "This is amazing," he said.

"Impressive," Mom agreed. Then she sighed. "Now how are you going to get my good pan off the fridge?"

I couldn't believe she was worried about a pan when her son had just created the world's strongest glue. "Mom, a simple 'Parker, you're a genius' will do," I informed her.

It was our first day sharing the room at the senior center, and it was going *so* well. My Golden Chords and I were dancing and singing while Maddie and her Silver Steppers worked out in the corner. True, they were a little more crowded than the day before, but we were all together, which was way more fun!

"I'm gonna strap on my Velcro shoes and dance with the Golden Chords, sing with the Golden Chords, jam with the Golden Chords. So turn up your hearing aids and come see the Golden Chords!" we sang loudly. I was so proud of them! They were projecting so well that I couldn't even hear Maddie's boring workout playlist.

"Break it down, Baxter," I cried at the end of the verse.

Then we all danced in the background while Baxter stepped forward and started rapping.

"Still got my teeth, still got my hair, my funky tight suspenders give me lots of flair. Come on, lady, I'm coming up atcha. I'm a gray-haired rapper whose handle is Baxtah. Word." Baxter dropped his cane like it was a microphone. Then he stumbled. "Wait, I need that," he called.

I hurried forward and picked up his cane for him.

Maddie suddenly marched over to me. "Liv, this just isn't going to work. You've got us squeezed into the corner tighter than Budge's workout pants."

"If you've got it, flaunt it, honey," Budge called from behind her.

"If you've got it, I've never seen it," Baxter countered.

"It's my room and I call dibs," Maddie said sternly. I was floored. I thought this was working out so well. Why was she being so dramatic? That was usually my thing!

"Dibs? Really? Are we a couple of first graders?" I scoffed. Then I added sarcastically, "Should we settle this with a game of dodgeball? Winner gets the room?" My Golden Chords stood behind me in solidarity.

Just then, a dodgeball came flying from Maddie's corner of the room and hit me in the stomach. It knocked the breath right out of me.

"Yes," hissed Budge.

"Nice shot, Budge," Maddie congratulated her.

Oh, no—no one throws a dodgeball at Liv Rooney and gets away with it, not even some cute little old lady, and certainly not with my twin sister and supposed best friend cheering her on. I stepped forward until I was inches away from Budge. "You should have stuck with canasta, granny," I said threateningly. "'Cause this game's gonna hurt." I wasn't sure what had gotten into Maddie, but if she wanted a fight, I was happy to give her one.

Joey

Now this was the way to be a Paulie protector! Skippy and I were both stone-cold chillin' in our Adirondack chairs, sipping frosty lemonade and feeling totally relaxed. Until Diggie came running around the corner looking utterly panicked.

"What is wrong with you two?!" he demanded.

I jumped to my feet. "What's wrong? What's wrong?" I asked.

Skippy was equally panicked. "Did you see sharks? Did you see sharks?"

"No! But I'll tell you what I did see: a giant bronze porcupine statue swinging upside down from a tree. When I was three blocks away!" Diggie yelled, gesturing to Paulie overhead.

We all looked up. "Okay, that is a problem," I said, rubbing the back of my head. "But you have to admit, when you're standing right here, you don't see him at all."

"We have to get him back! If people find out you took him, you'll be outcasts," Diggie responded. "And I'll be the doofus who picked the outcasts. And I am not going to be Diggie the doofus."

"Okay, okay," I said, trying to calm him. "Let's get him down."

I started walking to the tree slowly.

"Take your time, Joey," Diggie said sarcastically, and then he screamed, *"Go!"* He sure seemed mad.

I hurried over to the tree. "You two get under Paulie. I'm going to let him down slowly," I told them. I pulled at the knot holding Paulie up, but it was stuck. I gave it a good yank, and it came loose so quickly that I didn't have time to catch the rope. Paulie crashed to the ground and landed right on top of Dad's new grill with a sickening crunch.

"Dad's grill!" I yelled.

"Paulie!" Diggie wailed.

"My lemonade!" Skippy moaned.

Both Paulie and the grill were broken into pieces—too many to count—and Skippy's lemonade was nowhere to be seen. We were in such deep trouble.

Just then, Parker zoomed up on his scooter. Despite his having broken it the day before trying to fit eight kids on it at once, it looked good as new.

"Greetings, losers. And Diggie. Fixed my scooter," Parker called.

"Beat it, Parker," I snapped. "We have to figure out how to—wait a second, how'd you get that scooter back together?"

Parker pulled a jar filled with bright yellow goop out of his bag. "My new invention, Parker Paste, patent pending. Sticks to anything. I just glued Dad's toilet seat shut, so after dinner, get ready for the show!"

Parker Paste, huh? I thought. "Parker, your paste is the one thing that could get me out of this jam. I beg of you as your brother, please, give me some glue," I pleaded.

Parker laughed maniacally. "I think what we have here is what you'd call a *swap*-portunity."

A few minutes later I was holding the jar of Parker Paste and Parker was wearing Diggie's letterman jacket, holding my metal detector, and sipping our last lemonade.

"Pleasure doing business with you, butt bags." Parker laughed and took a big sip of lemonade. "Diggie, you're better than this." Diggie hung his head in shame.

Maddie

It was going to be a good old-fashioned dodgeball throw down. Winner got the room, and there was no way I was losing to Liv. It was my room first, and she needed to back off. Liv and I stood nose to nose. I had my Silver Steppers behind me, and she had her Golden Chords behind her. We were all holding balls and ready to play.

"This is no-holds-barred dodgeball. Winner takes the room. Loser takes—who cares? You're the loser," Baxter announced.

"You sure you want to do this, songbird?" I goaded Liv. "Jazz hands can't save you here."

"Oh, I'm sure," Liv assured me. "That ditch put ice in my veins—and a rash on my ankle." She actually looked pretty tough for once. For a moment, I wondered if I should be nervous. Nah . . . this was Liv we were talking about.

Budge blew a whistle, and the game began. She yanked off her clip-on earrings and charged into the fray, letting balls fly. Baxter threw balls two at a time while soft-shoeing, until he dropped his cane and got pummeled by the Silver Steppers. A Golden Chord hid behind the piano and used it as a shield. She would pop up every few seconds with a new ball to throw. Another Stepper used a purse filled with tissues and candy to block the shots.

Finally, the seniors were all out of the game. It was down to just Liv and me—and Liv was out of balls. It was the moment of reckoning. I threw the perfect shot, right at her stomach, but she grabbed Baxter's cane and hit the ball away. It sailed through the air . . . and right through a window, breaking it. There was a loud shattering sound. Liv and I froze, and then everyone else scuttled away as fast as their walkers could go. We were in so much trouble.

"Whoa," I said, staring first at the window and then at Liv.

Liv giggled nervously. "You know what, Maddie?" she said, twisting a curl around her finger. "Changed my mind. Room's all yours. See ya!" Then she ran for the door, leaving me alone to face the music.

Liv

That evening Maddie and I sat next to each other on the couch facing one very angry mom.

"Do you have any idea how it feels to have to pick up your daughters because they started a dodgeball riot at the senior center?" she lectured, hands waving as she paced back and forth. "No, you don't. Because it's never happened before in the history of the world."

"High marks for originality. What-what?" I said weakly, trying for a joke, but Mom was not in the mood.

"Because of you, the senior center will no longer allow my Ridgewood students to volunteer," Mom continued, ignoring my joke altogether. Hey! It hadn't been *that* bad.

Maddie looked down at the floor and said, "We're really sorry we messed it up."

"I swear, if we could fix it, we would," I added.

"Funny you should say that. Because I just happen to have two openings," Mom said with an evil little grin. Then she pulled out two neon-orange vests for the Beautify Wisconsin project.

"Not the ditch!" I wailed. How was I supposed to stay glamorous with trash in my hair and the stench of cattle on my clothes?

Mom nodded. "I signed both of you up for double the hours. Report to mile marker thirty-five, in between the cow farm and the sewage plant. What-what?!" Then she handed us the vests and headed into the kitchen.

"Dibs on the cow farm side," Maddie said, elbowing me playfully.

"Cute that you think there's a good side," I grumbled back at her, then sighed. Maddie and I needed to have a real talk—no dodgeballs involved. "So . . . what happened back there?" I asked seriously.

Maddie sighed. "I guess, just"—she played with her

charm bracelet, the way she always did when she was nervous—"the senior center was kind of my hang. You sort of space-invaded it."

Oh! Well, that certainly explained things. I just wished she'd told me how she felt. I had *no clue*—I must have lost some of my Maddie radar. I should have noticed that she was feeling too crowded. I thought it would be fun to volunteer together, but if she didn't, I could have always found something else to do. I guess we were both still adjusting to living together again after so long apart.

"Got it," I said. "Hey, here's an idea: next time something's bothering you, maybe say something before the over-eighty crowd opens a can of butt whup on us. Are we good?"

She laughed. "Yeah, we're good." Then she shook her head. I could tell she felt silly for not just being honest with me. I guess I hadn't totally lost my Maddie radar!

I stood up and was heading toward the kitchen when, suddenly, a dodgeball hit me in the back.

"Seriously?" I exclaimed, whipping around.

Maddie laughed. "No way I'm losing any sport to you."

That was it. I picked up a ball and aimed it at her. But I missed.

"You throw like a girl," she taunted, and threw the ball back. I ducked and then hurled one at her, hitting her smack in the chest.

"What-*what*?" I taunted back.

Joey

Well, it took all night, but that Parker Paste was amazing. We put Paulie back together and fixed my dad's barbecue. Oh, and somehow a spatula got stuck to my elbow. We got Paulie back to school and in his usual spot the next morning right before the big game against the Tiger Sharks.

"All right, Porcupines!" Diggie announced to the crowd of fans waiting in the hallway to watch the game. "We made it to game day and Paulie is safe and sound!"

The crowd cheered loudly.

Then Diggie pulled out two long links of bratwurst and held them out to Skippy and me.

"Gentlemen, your ceremonial bratwurst to bestow upon Paulie."

Skippy and I stepped forward and bowed. Diggie placed the sausages around our necks like medals.

"All right, do the honors," Diggie said, gesturing toward the giant Paulie statue.

Now it was our turn. We took the bratwurst links over to Paulie and placed them around his shoulders as the crowd cheered and clapped. We stepped aside.

"Okay, big finish," I told Skippy. Then we both unzipped our hoodies to reveal our supercool T-shirts. "Boo-yah!" we yelled in unison.

But the crowd didn't cheer—they laughed. I looked down and realized we were in the wrong order. "Oh, no, we're yah-boo," I wailed. "We're yah-boo! Switch! Switch!" We hurried to swap places and then yelled, "Boo-yah!"

But no one was looking at us. They were all focused on Paulie.

The statue had broken into a hundred pieces again under the weight of all the bratwurst. The crowd was not pleased.

I grabbed Skippy and started edging away. "Uh, go Porcupines?!" I yelled. Then we both turned and sprinted out of there as the crowd of basketball fans booed us.

Parker

That evening Dad fired up his new grill for its first use. Joey watched nervously, waiting for the grill to collapse, just like the Paulie statue had. Joey was basically the laughingstock of the school. I wish I could have seen it.

"Joey, my firstborn son," Dad said proudly, slinging one arm around Joey's shoulders. "It means a lot to me that you're here for the maiden burn of the Fire Magic Smokehouse Deluxe. Someday, all this will be yours."

"Yeah, yeah, that's great, Dad," Joey said, his voice all shrill and nervous. "Grill's all right, though, right? Any whiffs of burning glue?"

"It's fine. Why are you being so weird?" Dad asked.

I glided over to Joey on my scooter, his metal detector slung over my shoulder. He grabbed me and pulled me aside while Dad fussed with the meat.

He looked so relieved to see me. "Oh, thank goodness. I was worried about Parker Paste after the Paulie fiasco. But if your scooter's still in one piece, it appears Dad's grill will be okay," he said hopefully.

I laughed. "No, my other scooter broke again. This is a new one. Parker Paste is a total bust. But I made some adjustments to the metal detector. Now it detects fear." I held the metal detector up in front of Joey and made a loud beeping noise. "*Mehhhhhhhhhhhh.*"

"Hey, guys, does it look like rain?" Joey asked. He was freaking out. "Sure does. Cancel the barbecue! Everyone inside," Joey urged.

"What are you talking about?" Dad asked, looking at us like Joey had gone crazy. "You're about to taste what a two-thousand-dollar grill can do to a piece of meat."

"It cost *how* much?!" Mom demanded, walking out just then.

Now it was Dad's turn to be nervous. "Let's not get

sidetracked," he said, grabbing the empty platter out of her hands. "Time to take a look at these bad boys." He reached out to open the grill, but the entire thing collapsed at that moment, leaving only the handle in his hand.

"How did this happen?!" he shouted. Joey was going to be in so much trouble.

I held the metal detector up to Joey again and pretended to scan him. *"MEHHHHHHHHHHHH!"* I beeped.

TEAM LIV AND MADDIE

DOUBLE TROUBLE

• • • • •

Stay tuned for the next
snap-tastic Liv and Maddie book!